ID670162

Busy O'Brien and the Caterpillar Punch Bunch

Also by Michelle Poploff

Busy O'Brien and the Great Bubble Gum Blowout

Busy O'Brien and the Caterpillar Punch Bunch

Michelle Poploff

Illustrations by Judith A. Mitchell

Walker and Company   New York

Copyright © 1992 by Michelle Poploff
Illustrations © 1992 by Judith A. Mitchell
All rights reserved. No part of this book may be reproduced or
transmitted in any form or by any means, electronic or mechanical,
including photocopying, recording, or by any information storage and
retrieval system, without permission in writing from the Publisher.

All the characters and events portrayed in this work are fictitious.

First published in the United States of America in 1992
by Walker Publishing Company, Inc.

Published simultaneously in Canada by Thomas Allen & Son
Canada, Limited, Markham, Ontario

Library of Congress Cataloging-in-Publication Data
Poploff, Michelle.
Busy O'Brien and the caterpillar punch bunch / by Michelle
Poploff.
p.   cm.
Summary: Busy O'Brien works hard campaigning for her friend Mr.
Ficken to win the town's Good Neighbor of the Year Contest, aware
that her rival Jolly Van Pelt has entered her aunt.
ISBN 0-8027-8151-9
[1. Neighborliness—Fiction.   2. Contests—Fiction.   3. City and
town life—Fiction.]   I. Title.
PZ7.P7957Bs   1992
[Fic]—dc20   91-33838
CIP
AC

Printed in the United States of America

2   4   6   8   10   9   7   5   3   1

With love to my husband, Jeff,
my major source of everything

Contents

1

The Greatest Neighbor

W e're going to win. I can feel it in my bones," I said to Mitch and pedaled faster.

Mitch nodded. "Today is definitely our day," he said, pulling his bicycle ahead of mine.

Mitch Cotton, Rowena Cavendish, and I stopped our bikes in front of the gigantic yellow sign. Gravel crunched under our tires.

1

The sign said IS YOUR NEIGHBOR OUT-STANDING?

Roe read it out loud and looked at us.

I reached under my bicycle helmet and rubbed my itchy earlobe. "You better believe it," I said.

Mitch grinned. "We've got this contest locked up."

I quickly read the rules for probably the hundred and seventh time that week.

1. **Enter Mayview's Good Neighbor of the Year Award Contest.**
2. **If your neighbor is chosen, you'll win 30 free ice cream cones and can name a new Flavor of the Month at Last Licks Ice Cream Parlor.**
3. **The Good Neighbor of the Year will receive an award from Mayor O'Brien on Good Neighbor Day.**

4. All entries must go to the Community Events Office at Town Hall by 6:00 P.M. on May 16.

I could taste that ice cream already. Sweet, cold drops slipping down my throat. I closed my eyes. Double Fudge Delight here I come. "I could sure use some of that ice cream now," I said.

"Same for me," Mitch said, licking his lips. "I can't wait to sink my teeth into Pistachio Paradise." He sighed.

Roe took off her blue bicycle helmet. She blew her blond bangs out of her eyes. "What are we waiting for?" she asked. "Let's bring our poem into the Town Hall."

"Wait a minute," I said. "Let's show it to Mr. Ficken first. It will only take a few extra minutes."

"But we're already here," Mitch said.

"Come on," I said. "Mr. Ficken's always doing extra stuff for us. He deserves to know we chose him."

"Busy's right," Roe said. "Even when he's in a hurry, Mr. Ficken stops to fix a bike or skateboard on the spot." Roe rubbed her helmet. "I bet a lot of people don't know how important he is to Mayview."

"You're right," Mitch said. "Remember when he came to assembly and talked about fixing all kinds of things? That was the greatest day of school." He scratched at a scab on his elbow. "Let's go."

Roe strapped on her helmet, and we rode toward Main Street.

I looked at the heart-shaped sheet of stationery in my bicycle basket.

The poem about our good friend and neighbor Fred Ficken was perfect. And true. By now I knew it by heart. I said it out loud, and Roe and Mitch joined in.

Mr. Ficken is a really great man
When something is broken
He'll fix it if he can
He helps grown-ups and kids
He never minds the labor
He's everybody's friend
And the best kind of neighbor.

I patted the poem in my basket so it stayed safe and snug.

"I hope Mr. Ficken likes our poem," Roe said.

"The judges better like it," Mitch said. "That's what counts."

I looked at my friends who were riding on either side of me.

"That's for sure," I said. My throat felt so dry. "Are you two as thirsty as I am?"

"Definitely," Roe said.

I wiped my sweaty forehead. "We'll get something cold at my house after we get everything done."

5

"Sounds great," Mitch said. He began whistling.

While riding I thought about Mr. Ficken's white, bushy mustache and how it stretched across his face when he smiled. I figured it would stretch pretty far when he saw our poem.

We rode toward his shop, which is the sixth store on Main Street. Ficken's Fix-It Shop has a bright blue door with a blue-and-white-striped awning overhead.

Usually Mr. Ficken works outdoors when it's warm. I stood up in my seat to check. He was bent over an upside-down baby carriage.

Roe and Mitch rode a little ahead of me. I sat down and balanced on my seat, keeping my arms straight out on both sides.

From out of nowhere another bike

appeared. It was a flashy silver one that came straight toward me.

Turn, Busy, I told myself, as I grabbed the handlebars and tried to brake. Too late. The silver bike hit me. I crashed into the bike rack outside the Fix-It Shop. I felt as though the ground was rushing up at me.

Roe screamed my name. Something hit my chest.

Accidentally on Purpose

"Arrgh," I said.

Mr. Ficken helped me to my feet.

Mitch grabbed my bike.

I took off my red helmet and shook my head a few times. My jeans were ripped across both knees. Rats. There was blood running down my shirt. Blood. I jumped back. Then I saw it wasn't blood but ice cream. I felt my face get hot.

9

"Are you okay, Busy?" Mitch asked.

"I guess," I said, running my finger across my shirt.

"Raspberry Riot," Jolly Van Pelt said, coming toward me. She had an empty ice cream cone in her hand.

It would be Jolly Van Pelt who would cause a crash and make me look dumb. Stuck-up Jolly and her fancy silver bike.

Her friend Herbie "Boom Boom" Cannon got off his bike and checked Jolly's. "Not one scratch," he said.

"I didn't think so," Jolly said.

"This yours, Busy?" Boom Boom asked, picking up the lavender paper. It was splotched with Raspberry Riot ice cream.

"Our poem is ruined," Roe said, taking it from him. "We should have brought it in first thing." Her cheeks

10

puffed up. She looked ready to cry. "Now what do we do?"

Jolly reached into her pocket. She pulled out a pink tissue. "Will this help?" she asked.

"You know it won't," I said.

Mr. Ficken went into his store. He brought out some awful smelling ointment that he smeared on my scraped knees.

He chuckled, and his mustache stretched. "You certainly make a grand entrance, Busy O'Brien," he said. "No broken bones, I take it."

"I guess not, Mr. Ficken," I said, stretching my arms and legs.

He took the first-aid kit back inside just as Boom Boom pushed Jolly forward.

"Sorry, Busy," she said, looking at the ground. "I don't know what happened. I saw Mitch and Roe coming, but

Roe was sort of blocking you." Jolly stretched her hands out wide. "You know what I mean."

"Oh sure," I said. "You mean it's all Roe's fault."

"Kind of," Jolly said. "But not exactly."

"Save it, Jolly. I don't believe you for one second," I announced.

She dumped her empty cone into the trash can. "I don't see why you're complaining. I didn't even get to taste my ice cream," she said.

That did it. I caught some drips hanging on the hem of my shirt. "You want some? Why didn't you say so?" I said, leaning over. "I've got plenty."

Jolly quickly stepped back. "Very funny," she said, tossing her head. Every strand of her wavy blond hair was held in place by two large, silver barrettes.

"You can easily buy another cone," I said. "It took us hours to think up a good neighbor poem about Mr. Ficken. Now it's destroyed. Plus I used my best handwriting."

"And my last piece of stationery," Roe said.

"Well, it took me a lot of time to paint a poster of my aunt Ingrid with the flowers in her nursery. I entered her in the Good Neighbor Contest," Jolly said. "Herbie and I just came back from Town Hall."

"The deadline isn't till six o'clock. You still have time," Boom Boom said to Roe.

"But it would be a rush job," Jolly said. "I think you should forget about entering. There's always next year."

"Who cares what you think, Jolly," I said. "Mr. Ficken is the best neighbor in Mayview. He deserves the Good Neighbor of the Year Award."

"And when he gets it, we'll get free ice cream," Roe said.

Mitch nodded. "And our own flavor of the month."

"No way," Boom Boom said. "Me and Jolly are getting the free ice cream. First thing I'm getting is the Seven Scooper Cone."

My heart started thumping. That ice cream was ours. We worked hard for it. "The voting isn't until tomorrow, Jolly," I said. "Don't be so sure of yourself."

"You don't scare me," she said. "My aunt Ingrid's got the competition licked."

Boom Boom laughed loudly.

We didn't.

My head felt hot from arguing. My chest felt cold from the ice cream that was seeping through my shirt. "I can't go home looking like this," I said. "A reporter might be waiting around. You know, they're always trying to see if anything exciting is happening at the Mayor's house."

"Just be sure and tell your mother this was an accident," Jolly said, pointing to my clothes.

My mother, Helen O'Brien, is the Mayor of our town.

"Maybe she'll send you to jail," Roe said. A small smile came to her lips.

Jolly's mouth opened wide. "She can't do that. It was an accident." She stamped her foot.

"Sure, we know," I said.

"Well it was," Jolly said, climbing on her bike. "I still say you should give up," she called over her shoulder.

"And I say mind your own business," I called back.

Boom Boom waved to Roe and rode away with Jolly.

"I think Boom Boom likes you," I said to Roe.

"He sure has a funny way of showing it," she said. "He's always hanging around with Jolly and taking her side."

"Speaking of funny," Mitch said, pointing to my shirt, "Raspberry Riot is definitely your color, Busy."

"It would have looked better on Jolly," I said. "I'm going inside to wash up. Be right back."

The telephone rang inside the shop. Mr. Ficken coughed loudly.

"Are you all right?" I asked.

Mr. Ficken cleared his throat and nodded.

Mom will hate these ripped jeans, I thought while scrubbing my face. I hope no one sees me on the way home. Why can't I have a normal mother like

17

my friends? Roe's mother gives manicures at the beauty parlor. She's always bringing home sample polishes. Mitch's mom teaches high school English. She's home every afternoon and all summer. But what's the use of wishing? I blew my nose and turned off the bathroom light.

Mr. Ficken's back was to me. I didn't mean to listen in on his telephone conversation. But I couldn't help it.

"Yes, Dr. Kugel," he said. "The lab tests . . . stay in the hospital . . . surgery." Mr. Ficken coughed again. Oh boy. Mr. Ficken is sick, I thought. Really sick. And all we'd been thinking about was free ice cream. I couldn't listen anymore. I looked at my watch. I wished I could ask Mr. Ficken if he needed our help. But this probably wasn't a good time. Besides, we had to write our poem again. It was lucky we knew it by heart. I tapped Mr. Ficken's shoulder. "Thanks," I said. "See you soon."

He waved good-bye.

When I got outside I took the soggy poem from Roe. It was totally ruined. I crumpled it up and jammed it in my back pocket. "Wait till you hear about Mr. Ficken," I told my friends. "We've really got to beat Jolly."

Caterpillar Punch, Anyone?

We parked our bikes by the side of the red shed in my back-yard. Mom keeps saying the shed needs a new coat of paint. Dad bought some two months ago. He hasn't taken it out of the car yet.

"I'll grab another shirt and get us a drink," I said. "Then we'll do the poem again." I turned toward the house.

"I've got stuff to drink," a squeaky voice said.

I saw my younger next door neighbor, Gilbert "The Brat" Bratski, walking into our yard. He was pulling his red wagon. Inside was a green plastic pitcher and a box covered with netting.

I sighed. I was hot and sticky, and my knees stung. Gilbert's bright orange hair was sticking up on his head. The freckles on his face matched his hair. It's not that I don't like Gilbert. It's just that he has a certain way of inviting himself over when I'm with my friends.

"Hello, Gilbert," Roe said.

"Hi there," Gilbert said. "What's up?"

"How did you know we were here?" I asked him. "We didn't ride past your house."

"Easy," he said. "I saw you through my telescope, and then . . ." His eyes bugged out. "Hey, Busy, you're bleeding all over the place."

21

"It's not blood," I said, feeling tired. "It's Raspberry Riot ice cream."

"Busy and Jolly had a fight," Mitch said.

"Shucks," Gilbert said, slapping his thigh. "I miss all the good stuff." He put his hands on his hips. "Did she beat you up?"

"It wasn't like that," I said. "Our bikes bumped. I lost my balance, and her ice cream fell on me."

"Phooey," Gilbert said. "That's no big deal. You got any cups?"

I looked down at him. "Is this your way of getting to stay?"

"It's my drink," he said, wrapping his arms around the pitcher. Some of the brownish green drink sloshed out.

"Okay." I was too pooped to argue anymore. "I'll be right back." I fished around in my pocket for my key and unlocked the door.

Inside I quickly changed into another T-shirt. Then I got some cups and grabbed some blue stationery from Mom's drawer. It was the best I could find on short notice.

I ran outside and flopped onto the grass. "Pour the punch," I said. "I'm thirsty."

"You forgot to say the *P* word," Gilbert said.

"Please," I said to Mitch.

"What is this yucky looking stuff anyway?" Roe asked.

"Just drink stuff," Gilbert said.

I smelled it. "Stinky drink," I said, making a sour face.

"But it's cold," Mitch said, feeling the pitcher. He pushed his glasses farther up his nose.

Roe giggled. "Did you make it yourself, Gilbert?"

"Sort of," he said. He took off his

sneakers and wiggled his toes in the grass. "Stinkie feets," he said, sticking his feet in front of Roe's face.

Roe started laughing and couldn't stop. Then she began hiccuping.

"Not again," I said.

Sometimes when Roe laughs she gets the hiccups. Not always. But most of the time.

"Excuse me," Roe said, hiccuping again. She laughed. "Sorry, I can't help it." She hiccuped again, and some punch spilled out of her cup and onto Mom's stationery.

I crumpled it up. "I'd better not sit near you, or I'll never get this finished."

We picked up our cups and drank.

Mitch coughed. "What's in here?" he sputtered.

"This tastes like cough medicine," I said.

"That's why I'm coughing," Mitch said, slapping his knee.

Roe drank every drop. "I like it," she said. "Tastes kind of fruity." Her mouth formed into a big O.

"What?" I asked.

"Look, no hiccups," she said. "Gilbert's punch cured them."

I looked at Gilbert.

He didn't seem to care about Roe's hiccups. He was opening the box with the netting.

"What's in there?" I asked.

"Caterpillars," he said. "I'm collecting them."

"That's neat," Mitch said. "Caterpillars like chewing plants." He handed Gilbert a small leaf. "See if they'll eat this."

I shivered a little. "They remind me of green worms with fur on them," I said.

"Mr. Fishbane, our science teacher, said butterflies begin their lives as caterpillars. They hatch from eggs," Roe said. She filled our cups again.

"Oh boy," Gilbert said, tapping the little box. "Will my caterpillars turn into butterflies?"

"I guess so," I said. "But it takes time."

"Speaking of time," Mitch said, "you'd better write our poem again."

I nodded and finished my drink. "Hmm," I said, biting into something chewy and sweet. "Raisins?" I asked Gilbert.

He nodded. "But pretend they're bugs," he said, leaning toward me.

Mitch slapped Gilbert's back. "Thanks for the drink, I think," he said. "It was weird, but pretty cool."

"And it cured my hiccups," Roe said.

Gilbert scratched his head. "Next

time I'll use more caterpillars. Definitely," he said.

"Huh," I said, staring at him.

Roe started shaking.

Mitch clutched his stomach.

I pressed my finger to my throat.

"You mixed caterpillars into that punch?" Roe said.

"That's gross, Gilbert," Mitch said, flicking his tongue in and out of his mouth.

"Why you little Bratski," I said, reaching for his arm.

Gilbert slipped out of my reach.

"Wait a second," he said. "All I did was mix a bunch of stuff from the fridge into the pitcher."

"Go on," I said.

"My caterpillars were crawling on the table."

"How many?" I asked.

He held up six fingers.

27

"Now you've got two," Mitch said.

Gilbert nodded.

"So," Roe said slowly, "maybe they're in there and maybe they're not."

Gilbert shrugged. "I'm not exactly sure."

"Cute, Gilbert, very cute," Mitch said. Mitch didn't look very cute at all. He looked very green.

Gilbert looked relieved. "See, Busy," he said. "Mitch thinks it's cute."

"Drinking green hairy worms is not cute," I said, shaking a finger at him. "Any more tricks and you're out of here."

"I'll be good," Gilbert said, picking at the grass with his toes. He kept his head down. I could tell he was trying not to laugh.

"Forget about it," Mitch said.

"Fine with me," I said. "I just want to finish this poem. Then I'll feel better."

"All I want to do is throw up. Then I'll feel better," Roe said, clutching her stomach.

"You can't throw up in the Mayor's backyard," I said, moving away.

"It's practically town property," Mitch said.

"Just take a deep breath and relax," I said, pulling out my pen.

Roe did, and it worked.

After a few minutes she looked like her old self again.

I stretched out on the grass and used my math workbook to lean on. The sun warmed my back. I tried to write carefully. Finally I sat back and checked my work.

Mitch looked over my shoulder. "It's great, Busy," he said. "Almost professional."

"Almost?" I said, punching his arm. "It's perfect, Mitch." I didn't think it looked as great as before. But I didn't say so.

He laughed. "You're right, it is perfect. No one can stop us now. That ice cream is ours."

"Yeah," we cheered, throwing grass into the air.

That's when Jolly Van Pelt and Boom Boom Cannon wheeled their bikes into the backyard.

"Stop what?" Jolly asked, leaning her bike against the fence. She marched over to us.

Boom Boom was right behind her.

Nothing Can Stop
Us Now

I hid the poem behind my back. "None of your business," I said.

"We rang the doorbell, but no one answered," Jolly said.

"That's 'cause we're out back," Gilbert said. He stuck out his tongue.

Jolly ignored Gilbert. She flipped back her shiny blond hair. Her silver horse earrings sparkled in the sunlight.

I patted my wavy brown hair and made sure it covered my boring ear-lobes. I wish I had pierced ears.

Once I asked Dad. He said to try again when I'm eighteen.

"What are you doing here?" I asked.

"I'm just checking to see how you're feeling, Busy," Jolly said. "I mean after that awful fall." She looked at my torn jeans.

"Fall, what fall? I forgot all about it," I said.

"Good, I'm glad it's no big deal," she said.

Boom Boom wiped his sweaty red face. "What are you all drinking?"

I looked at my friends.

"It's, uh, caterpillar punch," I said, liking the sound of it. "Yeah, caterpillar punch."

No one said a word.

33

"Never heard of it," Boom Boom said, coming closer.

Roe cleared her throat. "Gilbert made it," she said. "It's very refreshing. And it cures hiccups."

"I don't have hiccups," Boom Boom said.

"See, it's working already," Mitch said, shaking Boom Boom's hand.

"Huh?" Boom Boom said, looking at his palm.

Gilbert held the pitcher under Boom Boom's nose.

Boom Boom looked inside. "Are those really caterpillars swimming around in there?"

Gilbert made a big fuss of looking inside. "Looks like raisins to me," he said. "They're sweet, and crunchy too."

"Herbie," Jolly said, pointing to Gilbert. "Don't listen to Gilbrat. He's just a dweeb."

"My name is Gilbert," he said, his face turning red. His freckles stood out more than usual. "And don't you forget it, because I'm a very important person." He pointed a grubby finger at Jolly. "I'll get you in trouble if you don't watch out."

Mitch came to the rescue. "So how about that drink, Boom Boom? There's not much left, and you look like you need something cold."

"Watch out! It looks weird," Jolly said.

"Looks aren't everything, Jolly." Roe poured Boom Boom a cup of caterpillar punch.

"Jolly, we didn't offer you punch anyway," I said.

Boom Boom finished the punch in two big gulps.

He squirmed a little, rolled his head

35

around, and slapped his big stomach. "This is the life. I feel better already."

"Have some more," Roe said, taking his cup.

Boom Boom opened his mouth.

Jolly leaped toward him.

A big burp came out.

Jolly grabbed his arm. "No more punch," she said. "We have important things to do."

Jolly walked to her bike, then turned around and smiled. "Need help with your poem?" She pointed to the crumpled pieces of paper lying around. "At this rate you'll never get to Town Hall."

I grabbed the poem from behind my back and stomped over to Jolly. We were practically eye to eye. I looked up a little and saw my nose in her round silver barrette.

Neither of us moved an inch.

I shoved the poem in front of her

face. "Nothing's gonna stop us now," I said in a low voice. My lips barely moved.

"Just trying to be a good neighbor," she said sweetly.

Mitch came between us. "May the best man win."

"You mean the best woman," said Jolly. She swung her leg onto her silver bike and rode off.

Boom Boom burped his good-bye. "That caterpillar punch was the best. You should sell it."

Roe jumped up. "Way to go, Busy," she said. "You really stood up to Jolly today."

"You think so?" I asked.

"Yeah, Busy," Gilbert said. "Jolly's not so hot, even if she's prettier than you."

"That's it, Bratski," I said, pointing toward his house.

"Okeydokey. I've got to find more caterpillars anyway," he said, getting to
his feet. "See you soon, right?"

"How soon?" I asked.

Gilbert giggled. His top front tooth
was taking forever to grow in. "I'll surprise you," he said.

"Just what I need," I said, grabbing
the empty cups. "More surprises."

Gilbert was still hanging around. His
lower lip stuck out. I knew that look.

"What?" I asked.

He got right to the point. "Can I get
free ice cream when Mr. Ficken gets
the Good Neighbor Award?"

"Gilbert's a positive thinker," Roe
said. "That's a good sign."

"All right," I said. "But no Raspberry
Riot."

5

Punch and Peanut Brittle

The three o'clock bell rang. Another day of school was over.

"Don't forget to study for the math quiz tomorrow," Ms. Lamb called out.

I grabbed my books. School was over at last. The Good Neighbor Committee was voting today.

I couldn't stop thinking about Mr. Ficken. What was wrong with him? I tried not to think about ice cream. Still, the taste of Chocolate Fudge Fripple and Marshmallow Malted wouldn't go away.

The committee just had to pick Mr. Ficken. And I knew one way to help them decide. I wouldn't even tell my friends. It would be a surprise.

When I passed Gilbert's house, he ran up to me.

"Look, Busy," he said. "I've got more caterpillars." He followed me up my back steps.

"Great," I said, opening the back door. In the kitchen I began pulling things out of the fridge.

"What are you doing?" he asked.

"I'm making a drink for the Good Neighbor Committee."

"I'll help," he said, slapping his hands together.

We grabbed everything that would fit

40

into the blender and stuffed it inside. I turned the blender on. It made a loud whirring noise. Gilbert covered his ears.

Some of the drink bubbled over. There were pits and stems and pieces of fruit all over the counter. No time to clean it up, though.

"That was fun," Gilbert said. "I like making messes at your house."

"I can see that," I said, opening the kitchen door. "Sorry, Gilbert, I've got to run."

"Okay," he said. "But, Busy."

"Huh," I said, fitting the lid on a pitcher. I shook it up a few times.

"My caterpillars are gone."

I groaned. Were they in the drink? There was no time to make more now. It was caterpillar punch or nothing. No one would know. I grabbed the pitcher and plastic cups.

When I reached Town Hall I saw Jolly locking her bike. I parked mine two slots down the row. My red bike looked ugly next to her silver speeder. Maybe I'll paint mine gold someday.

Jolly had a huge box of peanut brittle. She needed both hands to carry it. It looked gross.

"What are you doing here?" she asked.

"Same as you."

"I'm taking a snack to the Good Neighbor Committee," she said.

"Bribing the judges, you mean," I said, following her up the steps. "I should have known you'd do this."

"You're doing it too," she said. "But I thought of it first."

"Did not," I said. One cup slipped to the floor. I bent down. Jolly crushed it.

"Whoops," she said. "I didn't see it."

"Get some glasses," I said, walking ahead of her.

We bumped into my mother in the hallway. She was talking with a tall man with curly brown hair. Some reporters were following them.

Mom hugged me. "Busy, Jolly," she said. "This is a welcome surprise. Are you here to see me?"

"Well," I began.

"I'm just on my way into a meeting with the traffic commissioner, Mr. Buchwald."

My mother introduced us.

Jolly shoved her peanut brittle at me so she could shake hands with Mr. Buchwald.

Then I loaded her down with my cups, pitcher, and her peanut brittle, so I could do the same.

"I'll be right with you," Mom told Mr.

Buchwald and the reporters. They walked down the hall.

"Anyway." She smiled, turning to us. "It's nice to see you together."

"We're not really together," I said, balancing the pitcher and cups.

Jolly tried tucking the peanut brittle under her arm. "We just sort of met outside," she said.

"Oh, I see," said Mom.

"That's a lovely shade of red, Mayor," Jolly said. "It's perfect for your complexion."

"Thank you, Jolly," my mother said, pulling at a thread on her sleeve.

Mom did look nice in her new red dress. I wish I'd said so first.

"Well now, why are you here?" Mom asked.

There was no way to hide it. "I was on my way to the Community Events Office."

45

"Same for me," Jolly said.

Mom pointed to a bench in the hall. We sat down.

"What do you have there?" she asked, placing a large folder on her lap.

"Punch," I said.

"Peanut brittle," said Jolly.

Mom lifted the pitcher lid and looked inside. She wrinkled her nose.

"We figured the committee might want a snack," I said.

"You mean you're bribing the judges," Mom said, folding her arms.

Jolly and I looked at each other.

"Really, girls, you should know that's not allowed. It's not fair to the others who entered."

"It's not fair to let anyone drink that gross punch," Jolly said.

"They'll probably break their teeth on your peanut brittle," I said.

"Please, girls," Mom said, holding up

46

her hands. She drummed her fingers on the bench. "Tell you what," she said. "I'll take these refreshments in myself. I won't say who donated them." She took a sheet of blue stationery from her folder and wrote *Refreshments* on it. "There, how does that look?"

"That looks like the same paper Busy used for Mr. Ficken's Good Neighbor poem," Jolly said.

Mom looked over at me.

That Jolly.

I gulped. "It was the only nice paper around," I said. "Besides, it was an emergency."

"Busy, this is official stationery. It's not for you . . ." Mom stopped and swallowed. I guess she remembered Jolly was listening.

"We'll discuss this another time. I'll take these in now," she said. She stopped and looked at both of us. "Remember, girls, this isn't a major battle. This is all about being a good neighbor."

"Yes, Mayor," Jolly said.

"Can we wait here while they decide?" I asked.

"Absolutely not. The Good Neighbor of the Year Award will be announced in the morning paper. Now scoot," she said, throwing me a kiss. "And on behalf of the Committee, thanks for your contributions."

"You're very welcome, Mayor O'Brien," Jolly said. She shook Mom's hand.

"See you later, Mom," I said.

Mom took the snacks and walked away.

Jolly and I stood up together.

I stepped on her foot.

"Ouch," she said.

"Sorry," I said. "It was an accident."

"Sure," she said. Jolly's eyes were little slits.

I could tell she didn't believe me. I didn't care.

"Tattletale," I said, walking down the steps. "I didn't tell my parents about my ripped jeans and junked-up shirt. And I never told about the crash, which was your fault."

"This is different," Jolly said. "You used town property for your personal use. The Mayor has a right to know."

"It wasn't for me," I said. "It was for Mr. Ficken."

"Still," Jolly said.

I threw up my hands. It was no use explaining.

We took our bikes and rode off in opposite directions. When I looked over my shoulder, Jolly was out of sight. Excellent. I swung around and rode back to Town Hall.

Two seconds later Jolly rode into view. We headed toward each other and stopped tire to tire. No crash this time. No excuses. Just the sound of squeaky wheels. We sat down on the steps and waited.

I bit my nails.

Jolly cracked her knuckles.

Neither of us spoke for a long time.

Finally I couldn't stand it anymore.

"Doesn't anyone else care about the Good Neighbor of the Year Award besides us?"

She shrugged. "I was just thinking."

"About what?"

"My flavor of the month," she said. "I can't decide if I like Jolly Bean or Jolly Good."

Her flavor of the month. Pooh.

I hadn't even thought about what to

call our flavor of the month. I went back to my biting.

She kept cracking.

Nibble nibble.

Crack crack.

Suddenly we heard footsteps.

"It's about time," Jolly said.

We jumped up and turned around.

It was my mother.

"Uh oh," I said, ducking down.

"Did you girls forget something?" Mom called to us.

We shook our heads.

"Then for the last time, go home. Now."

We got on our bikes.

"I'm going to Last Licks to check out some flavors," Jolly said. "Maybe I'll invent something new."

"I have an idea," I said, strapping my helmet on. "It's perfect for you."

"What is it?" Jolly asked.

"Lemon onion," I said, stepping on the pedal. I didn't look back.

I rode straight home and tried studying for my math quiz. When I heard Mom come home, I waited awhile, then went downstairs. Maybe she would tell me who won.

When I walked into the kitchen, she whirled around.

"Busy," Mom exploded. "The entire kitchen is a mess."

I clapped my hand over my mouth. I'd forgotten all about it.

"Mr. Buchwald is waiting in the car. I was going to ask him in for coffee. It's a good thing I didn't."

"I'll clean this up in a jiffy, Mom," I said, grabbing a sponge.

"Never mind," she said, shaking her head. "We'll stop at the diner. Can't I rely on you to clean up after yourself?

"Honestly," she went on, "you're not a baby anymore."

I stared down at the floor, hoping I'd drop into the basement. My face burned. Mom was right. I'd let her down.

She grabbed some papers from the table. The top one had a strawberry smear on it. "And you had no right to take my stationery without permission," she added. "Tell your father I'll be home by ten."

I nodded as she walked out. The door slammed behind her.

Great. Now Mom was furious with me. I brushed some tears away from my eyes and cleaned up the kitchen. A caterpillar crawled in the sink. Yuck.

I watched it crawl out of the sink and onto the windowsill. Lucky caterpillar. No one yelled at him.

I didn't feel like studying anymore.

53

I'll never figure out long division anyway.

I went out and rocked on the porch swing. I pulled Dad's floppy beach hat over my head and put my feet up on the rails. If anyone passes by, I thought, they won't know it's me.

I closed my eyes and thought about Very Cherry Vanilla ice cream. That made me feel a little better. Not much. But a little.

It's Not Fair

L ast night Dad helped me study. He made things a lot easier.

We made chocolate pudding together. Then I went to bed early.

I don't know what time I fell asleep. It seemed to take forever. In my dreams Jolly was eating ten ice cream cones at once. Mom was giving her the Good Neighbor of the Year Award. I got stale peanut brittle. Gross.

The next morning Mom, Dad, and I sat at the breakfast table waiting for the morning paper. I was sitting next to Dad, across from Mom.

My throat felt tight and dry. I could hardly eat.

Mom and I looked at each other across the table.

"I'm sorry," we said at the same time.

"Yesterday was a long, hard day, Busy. I didn't mean to blow up at you," Mom said, pouring some coffee.

"I didn't mean to use your stationery. And I feel awful about the kitchen. I was in such a hurry."

Mom smiled. "I wouldn't recognize you if you weren't in a hurry. It's a new day," she said, reaching over for a hug. "Besides, the committee liked the punch. Of course, I couldn't tell them you made it."

That made me feel a little better. "Speaking of the committee, what happened?"

"Oh no you don't," Mom said. "I'm not telling."

"Please tell me something," I begged. "Anything."

Mom thought a minute. "Let's see," she said, adding milk to her coffee. "There is one thing."

"What," I said, leaning forward on the table. I could see my face in the coffeepot. It looked long and rubbery. I puffed up my cheeks.

"Mrs. Willoughby asked for the punch recipe. She said it tasted unusual."

I could guess why. "No fair, Mom," I said. I rolled my napkin into a ball and tossed it at her.

She ducked and laughed.

"Why won't you tell, Mom? I'm your

flesh and blood." I poured cornflakes into my bowl. A toy whistle fell out of the box. I blew it softly.

"You'll find out when everyone else in Mayview does," she said, sipping her coffee.

I turned to my father. "Do you know, Dad?"

"Are you kidding?" he said.

We heard a plop on the porch.

"Thank goodness," Dad said. "The suspense is over."

I ran to the door and grabbed the paper off the porch. The announcement was on page three.

I saw Mr. Ficken's name. "Yes," I yelled, raising my fist in the air. "We did it."

Then my eye caught another name. Ingrid Van Pelt. What? How could they?

"Well?" Mom said, when I walked back to the table.

"It's a tie," I said, dropping the paper on Dad's lap. "That's not fair."

"Says who?" Mom said. "I think it's terrific to have a male and female Good Neighbor of the Year. We'll give two awards."

I sank into my chair. My cornflakes were soggy. "I think it stinks. There should be one winner," I said.

Dad looked up from the sports page. "Why?" he asked.

I shrugged. "It's more special that way."

Dad put the paper aside. "It can be just as special with two people," he said, reaching for my hand.

"But Jolly's aunt Ingrid is so snobby. Jolly's just like her."

I looked at my mother. She was putting on lipstick. She used the little mirror she keeps in her purse. On the other side of the mirror is a picture of me in a green bathing suit. It was taken when I was five years old. Even younger than Gilbert.

"Mom?" I asked.

"Y-e-s," she said, stretching her mouth as she slid the lipstick back and forth.

"Are you sure the committee counted right? Maybe it wasn't really a tie and Ms. Van Pelt lost by one vote."

Mom snapped her purse shut. "Busy, I'm ashamed of you," she said, raising her voice. She blotted her lipstick on a napkin.

I picked it up and folded the napkin carefully. Her lip print might be famous someday.

Mom went on. "Ingrid founded Mayview's Garden and Culture Club. She does a lot for our town."

"You'll see," I said. "Jolly won't like this either."

"Jolly won't have anything to say," Mom said, reaching for the paper.

I dumped my bowl in the sink.

Mom turned around. "I thought you'd be thrilled. Mr. Ficken's getting the award. And you and your friends get free ice cream," she said. "Who could ask for more?"

Mom was right. Free ice cream for us. The award for Mr. Ficken. Mr. Ficken! I froze in my chair. I'd forgotten about him. He was very sick. My parents didn't know. No one knew. I had to go see him. I quickly rinsed my bowl and spoon.

"What's your flavor of the month going to be?" Dad asked.

I had other things on my mind. "Uh, I don't know," I said. "We didn't get that far."

The telephone rang. I jumped. Dad answered it. He listened for a few seconds, then handed the phone to Mom.

"It's Jolly Van Pelt," he said. "She's demanding a recount."

I shook my head. That copycat.

7

Count on Busy

After school Roe and I went to the Fix-It Shop. Mitch had a dentist appointment.

"Congratulations," we said, hugging Mr. Ficken.

"Come in," he said. "I need to talk with you."

Roe and I looked at each other.

"We want to talk with you too," I said.

Mr. Ficken's voice sounded hoarse,

and he looked tired. Even his mustache looked droopy, and his cheeks weren't their usual rosy color.

Roe and I sat on high stools behind the counter.

A square brown box caught my eye. "Is that what I think it is?" I asked, clasping my hands.

Mr. Ficken nodded. He was fixing my grandmother's music box.

"Hand me that screwdriver near the hammer, please, Busy," he said. "The small one with the black handle."

"Sure," I said, reaching over a bunch of tools.

"Rowena, could you pass me two screws from the green box in the middle drawer?"

"Sure thing," Roe said. The drawer was stuck. She gave it a few quick pulls, and it opened.

"Now, where did I put my pliers?" he said, scratching his head.

We looked around.

"Right here," I said, reaching to a nearby shelf.

"Ah ha," he said.

I licked my lips. "Mr. Ficken," I began. "I'm not exactly sure how to say this . . ."

Roe butted in. "What's wrong with you?" she asked. "You don't look so hot."

Mr. Ficken blew his nose. Then he smiled at us. "First, let me say how much I appreciate what you've done." He rolled up his sleeves. "But I can't accept the award on Sunday."

"What do you mean?" Roe asked. Her mouth hung open.

"I'll be in the hospital," he said. His hands shook a little.

I knew it had to be something horrible. "What's wrong?" I asked.

"I've had colds and coughs all winter. They've lasted into the spring. Now Dr. Kugel says I must have my tonsils removed," he said.

"I thought only kids got their tonsils out," Roe said.

Mr. Ficken nodded. "That's true most of the time," he said, while working. "Dr. Kugel says it's unusual, but it happens."

"Well I had mine out last year, and it's no big deal, so don't worry about it," Roe said, slapping his back.

"That's right," I said, feeling much better. "And you'll have to eat lots of ice cream. Your throat will be better in no time. By the way, what's your favorite flavor?"

"Butter pecan," he said. "But . . ."

"No buts, Mr. Ficken. Butter pecan's

going to be the flavor of the month," I said.

"Dipped in chocolate sprinkles," Roe said, rubbing her hands together.

"Perfect," I said. "And don't worry, we'll come up with an exciting new name for it."

"Even though there will be two flavors of the month, ours will be better," Roe said, banging the counter with the hammer.

We were so busy talking about ice cream I almost forgot about Mr. Ficken's problem. His head was bent over Grammy's music box. His hair looked like a bunch of gray cotton balls stuck together.

"Can't you get your tonsils out after the ceremony at Town Square?" I asked.

He shook his head. "I'm afraid not.

Dr. Kugel is going on vacation. It must be done now," he said.

"But that's not fair," I said. "It's your award."

"And our ice cream," Roe said, jumping off the stool.

I looked at her.

"Well it is," she said.

I felt exactly the same way.

"Now what do we do?" Roe asked, rolling a screwdriver toward me.

I turned the screwdriver around in my hand while Mr. Ficken worked. He was a good friend. We had to do something, but what?

I looked at Mr. Ficken. We brought things to him that were old or broken, like Grammy's music box. Everything he gave back was at least a little bit better than before.

Now it was our turn to give something back to him.

"If you can't come to the Good Neighbor Award Ceremony at Town Square, I'll find a way to bring it to you."

Mr. Ficken stopped working. He coughed and reached for his tea.

I patted his back.

Roe gulped. "How will you do that? What will your mother say?"

"Don't worry about my mother. I'll take care of it."

Mr. Ficken smiled his stretchy smile. "Don't get yourself into mischief on my account, Busy. I'd feel terrible."

"You know Busy. She isn't happy unless she's helping someone else," Roe said. She climbed up on the stool. "If Busy says you'll be there, then you can count on it."

Mr. Ficken laughed. "All right then. Keep me posted." He pushed the music box toward me. "Now let's give this a whirl."

I turned the key. It made a scratchy noise. I held my breath. The sweet sounds of "Danny Boy" filled the store.

The three of us smiled.

It was a good sign.

I felt sure my plan would work.

All I needed was a plan.

A Change for the Better

When I got home the house was quiet.

Dad might come in at any minute. He's an architect and does a lot of work at home.

There was no time to chicken out. I walked into the kitchen.

I took the telephone book and found Dr. Kugel's number. I took three deep breaths and dialed.

I was about to hang up when a man's voice said, "Dr. Kugel."

"Hello, I'm Elizabeth O'Brien."

"Yes," he said.

"I'm a friend of Fred Ficken's," I said. I quickly blurted out Mr. Ficken's problem. "Would it be all right if my mother gave the Good Neighbor Awards on the lawn of Mayview General this year? Then Mr. Ficken could be there. It means a lot to him, and it will only take a few minutes."

"Your mother," he said. "What's your name again?"

"Elizabeth O'Brien, but mostly everyone calls me Busy."

"I'm beginning to see why," he said. "I've seen your picture in the newspaper, and I've met your parents several times. Does your mother approve of this plan?"

"We're still working out the details," I said, biting my lip.

There was no sound for a few seconds. I held my breath.

"Then it's all right with me," he said finally.

"Whew." My breath came out in a rush.

"I'll admit I haven't been to a Good Neighbor ceremony for years," he said. "It's not very neighborly of me, but I'm always working."

"Now you can go," I said. "Thanks for your help."

"You're welcome," he said. "I'll see you on Sunday."

I hung up and took another deep breath. That was one down. I quickly called the newspaper to tell Mr. Marshall, a reporter, the news. He wasn't there, so I left a message.

Then I called Mr. Ficken, told him the plan, and wished him luck.

I felt so great I ran out back, grabbed my bike and helmet, and rode around the block.

The wind felt cool on my cheeks. The strong sunshine made all the houses look brighter. Even Mr. Scott's place, which was painted an ugly brown. He should paint his shutters white. I'll tell him next time I see him. I rode around three more times. Then I went inside to make a salad.

That night at dinner I brought Grammy's music box to the table.

"Busy," Mom said, "is it fixed?"

I nodded. "Mr. Ficken wanted to finish it before he went to the hospital. That's why he's such a terrific neighbor."

"So he is," Mom said, reaching for a slice of roast beef. "It's such a shame

he can't be at the awards ceremony." Mom passed the peas and carrots to me.

I quickly passed them on to Dad. Nobody noticed.

Mom continued. "What a time to get his tonsils out." She pointed her fork at me. "As soon as he gets back to the shop, I'll bring him his Good Neighbor Award myself."

Dad buttered his roll. "No need to do that, Helen. I was at the barber's and heard that the awards will be given at the hospital." Dad bit into his roll and smiled at Mom.

I gulped. News sure travels fast around here. I kept my head down and pretended to eat.

"Really," Mom said. "Actually, it's a terrific idea. Now Fred won't miss out. But I do wish people would clear these things with me first." She reached for her napkin and shrugged. "I was probably in a meeting when it happened. Seems the Mayor is always the last to know."

She turned to me. "Did you do anything special today, Busy?" she asked.

"Just the usual," I said, reaching for my water glass. I knew Mom would find out sooner or later. I figured I might as well get it over with, now. I cleared my throat.

"Would you excuse me?" Mom said. "I've had a headache all day. I think I'll go upstairs and take a hot shower." She took the music box and kissed the top of my head.

I'd have to find another time.

I couldn't eat anymore. "I'll load the dishwasher, Dad," I said.

After I finished I went upstairs to do homework. Suddenly I felt tired. I got undressed and washed up. "Good night," I called out. No answer.

Tossing in bed, I worried about not telling Mom about changing the ceremony to the hospital.

I got out of bed and tiptoed to my parents' bedroom. Dad was in the shower. This was the perfect moment to tell Mom.

I peeked into the room. Grammy's music box was playing on Mom's bedside table. Mom was fast asleep.

I sighed. Maybe tomorrow.

Another Fast Plan

The next day came and went. I didn't tell Mom. A part of me hoped I'd never have to explain. In a few more days Mr. Ficken would get his award and we would get our free ice cream. I thought I might start off with banana blueberry.

Everything was going great. At least that's what I thought.

After school Mitch, Roe, and I were

going to work on a science project at my house.

We snuck by Gilbert's on the way home. I looked up at his bedroom window. No telescope. No Gilbert. Yet.

When we got to my house he was sitting on the front steps. "Fooled ya," he said, waving at us.

I had to let him in.

We were sitting at the dining-room table. So far Gilbert was working quietly on a get well card for Mr. Ficken. It was his own idea.

"Guess what," he said. "My dad says I'm named for a famous relative." He rubbed his nose with a purple crayon. "That means I'll be famous too."

This was news to me. I looked up from tracing the planet Mars. "Who is the famous person?" I asked.

The doorbell rang.

"I'm not supposed to tell," Gilbert said, pinching his lips together.

"Why not?" Mitch asked.

The bell rang again.

I shrugged. "Be right back."

Jolly Van Pelt was standing on our porch holding a blue book.

"What do you want, Jolly?" I asked.

"You'll see," she said, pushing a book into my hands.

I felt trouble coming. "What is it?" I asked, trying not to sound nervous.

"It's a very special delivery," she said, giving me a phony smile.

It was *The History of Mayview*. Our copy was in Dad's office. "What's this for?"

"Forget about having the Good Neighbor of the Year Awards at the hospital," she said.

"No way," I said. "It's all set."

"Then you'll have to unset it," she

said, leaning against my door. "Read page twenty-five."

"Hold your horses and I will." I hoped my hand wasn't shaking.

By now Roe, Mitch, and Gilbert were at the door.

"It says the Good Neighbor Award is given in front of the Silas G. Mayview Statue," I said.

"That's at Town Square," Mitch said.

"But then Mr. Ficken can't go," Roe said to Jolly.

"Exactly," Jolly said. "Which means my aunt Ingrid will get the award by herself."

I had to think fast. "Hold on. That's not the only statue in town," I said.

"It's not?" Roe said, behind me.

I nudged her.

"Oh right, I forgot, it's not," she said, shaking her head.

"Where will you find another one?"

Jolly asked. "What will you do, make your own?" She laughed in my face.

Not a bad idea, I thought. I laughed back.

"You'll find out soon enough," I said, leaning closer to her.

She grabbed her book. "I'm leaving," she said.

"Don't come back." I slammed the door.

"You should have socked her one, Busy," Gilbert said, jumping around and throwing fake punches.

I smiled at my friends. "Guess what? Jolly doesn't know it, but she's just given me an idea."

"Another plan?" Roe asked, backing up.

"Come here," I said. "It's simple. We'll draw our own statue on gigantic paper and use it on Sunday."

"But that's not the same as the real statue," Roe said.

"The book didn't say anything about the original statue," I said.

Mitch groaned. "We're not good artists, Busy," he said. "Jolly's the best in school."

"You don't expect me to ask for Jolly's help," I said. "That's the last thing I'd do."

"I've got tons of crayons," Gilbert said. "Plus I draw good noses."

"Okay, you're in," I said. I couldn't be picky. "Bring any supplies you have at home. I'll ask Miss Kristen in art for a large roll of paper. Jolly's in for a big surprise."

Teamwork

The next afternoon we worked hard on the poster. But no matter what we did, it still looked strange.

"I can't believe you talked us into making our own statue," Mitch said, cleaning his glasses on his T-shirt.

"Neither can I," I said. "But we can't stop now."

"Stop what," Jolly said, as she and Boom Boom walked into my backyard.

"Not again," I said, shaking my head. "I told you not to come back."

"Well, we just happened to be in the neighborhood," Jolly said, "Besides, since my aunt is getting the award also, I have a right to see what you're doing."

She looked down and folded her arms. "Ugh, you call that art," she said, kicking at the corner of our poster. "Silas G. Mayview looks tacky. He'd die if he knew what you've done to him."

"He's already dead," Mitch said, adjusting his glasses.

Jolly tapped her toe. "And that horse looks ridiculous," she went on. "You can't even draw a horse's face."

"Hold still and we'll trace your face," Gilbert said.

Boom Boom snickered behind Jolly's back.

Jolly jabbed him in the side.

87

"Ha, ha," she said. "I'm only trying to help."

"No you're not," I said, rubbing my aching neck. "You're just being yourself. And quit kicking our stuff."

"Yeah," Roe said. "Too bad if you don't like it. We're doing our best."

"Well it's not good enough," Jolly said. "You can't let the town see this poster on Sunday. It's embarrassing. People will laugh."

"No they won't," I said. But what if she was right?

Jolly leaned closer. "Who gave Silas G. Mayview such a big nose?" she asked.

"I did that," Gilbert said, pounding his chest. "Neat, huh?"

"Noses are his specialty," Mitch said.

"That's great if you're drawing a clown, but not Mayview's founding father."

"That does it," I said. "We need to finish. Leave us alone."

Jolly just stood there.

"Busy means scram," Gilbert said, squinting up at Jolly.

"Thanks, Bratski," I said. "She knows what I mean."

"All right, I'm going," Jolly said, straightening up. "But don't say I didn't warn you."

"We won't," Mitch said.

"Besides, I wouldn't help you even if you begged me," Jolly said. "After all . . ."

"Anybody home?" a voice called out. Mr. Marshall, a reporter from the *Mayview Mirror*, walked into the yard. "Hello, kids," he said, waving to us. "How's your statue coming along?"

"We're not done yet, Mr. Marshall," I said, brushing grass out of my hair. We looked sloppy and sweaty. All except for Jolly, of course.

Mr. Marshall held up his camera.

"This doesn't look so hot," Mitch said. "I don't think you want a picture."

"No problem," Mr. Marshall said. "I'll call it a work in progress. I know just the spot for it in tomorrow's paper." He pulled out his notepad. "Are you part of this too, Jolly? The painting you did of your aunt was wonderful. You have real artistic talent."

Jolly turned red. It clashed with her pink top. First she looked at us. Then she looked at Boom Boom.

He nodded at her.

She bent down and turned the poster this way and that. Then she cracked her knuckles.

"Yes, Mr. Marshall. I'm part of this project. Can we have a few more minutes before you take the picture?"

"Sure thing," he said, making notes on his pad.

Jolly grabbed a marker and made some quick strokes.

I let out the breath I'd been holding in. It was true. Our poster did look weird. I didn't want Jolly's help. But I wanted our poster to look good.

"Remember," I whispered to Jolly. "We didn't ask for your help. Don't try and take over."

She pulled her hair into a ponytail. Her pink heart earrings jiggled. "Then you remember I didn't offer."

"You were just about to . . ."

"Was not," she said.

"Was too."

"Hmph," she said, bending over the poster. "I'll do the outline, and the rest of you fill it in."

Roe slid over, and Boom Boom sat down to help.

"She's so bossy," Roe said to me. "But she can draw."

I nodded and crossed my eyes.

Roe giggled and covered her mouth.

"Don't laugh," I said, squeezing her arm. "We don't have any caterpillar punch."

Roe pressed her lips together and waited. Nothing happened.

"I'm ready," Mr. Marshall said. "Everyone say ice cream."

"Ice cream," we shouted.

"Excellent," he said. "I'll call this picture 'Teamwork.' Thanks, kids. Be sure to look for your picture in the paper tomorrow." He packed up his gear. We waved good-bye.

Our teamwork paid off. We finished the poster by dinnertime.

Gilbert got some blue marker on Jolly's elbow.

"Accident," he said. He looked down and grinned.

"There've been a lot of those lately," Jolly said, rubbing at her elbow.

She looked at me.

I nodded. "You'd better go before we have another one."

She did.

11

A Knockout Punch

This was it. Mayview's Good Neighbor Day.

I felt all nervous and tingly inside.

The sun beat down hot and heavy. It felt more like summer than spring.

Crowds of people were walking toward Mayview General.

I could see it all. Mr. Ficken getting his award. Us getting free ice cream.

Chocolate Cherry Twist, here I come, I thought.

Jolly bumped my arm. "Come on, let's do it," she said.

We quickly hung the Silas G. Mayview poster over the entrance.

"Not bad," I said to her. "Thanks for helping."

She nodded. "I did it for my aunt Ingrid."

Jolly seemed sort of nervous too. She looked pale and kept touching her stomach. I figured it wasn't my business.

Our town colors are blue and yellow. A lot of people were wearing them. A man handed me a blue balloon and a yellow one for Jolly. She wore blue and yellow ribbons in her hair. If I tried that they'd fall out in a minute.

"Cute ribbons," I said.

She wiped her forehead.

I'd never seen her sweat before.

I couldn't stand it anymore. "I know it's not my business, but you look a little weird."

She shrugged. "I skipped breakfast, and now I feel dizzy."

"How about . . . ," I said.

"Oh Jolly," a voice called.

Jolly turned. "There's Aunt Ingrid. Don't tell her," she said. "Coming," she called.

That was okay by me. I walked toward Mr. Ficken. He was sitting in a wheelchair. I waved, and he smiled his stretchy mustache smile. I tied my balloon to his chair.

"You look good, Mr. Ficken," I said, leaning down for a hug.

"I'm on the mend," he said.

A tall man with gray hair held out his hand. "Hello, Busy, I'm Dr. Kugel."

We shook hands.

"Quite a crowd here today," he said.

I nodded, fanning my neck.

Someone touched my arm.

It was Gilbert with his wagon. Inside were two green pitchers and lots of paper cups.

"What's all that stuff for?" I asked.

"I'm selling caterpillar punch," he said. "It's only twenty-five cents a cup. Real cheap."

"You can't do that," I said.

"Can too," he said, his hands on his hips. "Famous people do whatever they want. Besides, it's hot out here." He walked past me. "Are you thirsty, Mr. Ficken? You can have some for half price."

"Gilbert Bratski," I said.

"All right," he said. "Free."

Before Mr. Ficken had looked pale. Now two bright spots glowed on his cheeks. He chuckled. "Thanks anyway,

Gilbert," he said. He reached over and rumpled Gilbert's already rumpled hair.

Gilbert pulled a folded card out of his sneaker. He handed it to Mr. Ficken. "I made it myself," he said.

"Thank you," Mr. Ficken said.

Roe came over and handed Mr. Ficken a pink bottle.

"Peeuw," Gilbert said, holding his nose. "What's that stinky smell?"

Roe looked upset. "It's strawberry foot lotion," she said. "It's very soothing."

"There's nothing wrong with Mr. Ficken's feet," Gilbert said. "It's his tonsils that were sick. You should have bought cough drops."

"My mother says it's the thought that counts," Roe said. She looked at Mr. Ficken.

Mr. Ficken cleared his throat.

"Thank you," he said. "This will come in handy. I'm on my feet a lot at the store." He put the bottle and card in his robe pocket.

My mother and Ms. Van Pelt walked over to us.

"We'll begin in a few minutes," Mom said, shaking hands with Mr. Ficken. "How are you, Fred?"

"This," he said, pointing to the crowd, "makes me feel much better."

Next to me Roe was looking into Gilbert's pitchers. "Did you put caterpillars in the punch this time?" she asked.

He giggled. "I'm not telling," he said.

"Then I'm not buying," she said, rolling back on her heels.

"You'll be sorry," he said.

Then, as my mother called the crowd to order, I saw Gilbert pull a little box out of his pocket. I froze as he pulled off the top and let the caterpillars loose in his wagon.

Some were crawling around the cups. Others crawled toward the pitchers.

The crowd was quiet.

I couldn't move.

Mom welcomed everyone to the Good Neighbor of the Year Award ceremony. Applause sounded. Hurry up, Mom, I begged silently. Then she thanked the hospital staff. More clapping. More caterpillars. There must have been a dozen. I had to get to Gilbert.

Mom talked on. "And Dr. Kugel just told me that when he and Mr. Ficken were out here earlier this morning, Mr. Ficken noticed a faulty sprinkler system on the lawn. So as a result of holding the awards here today, Mr. Ficken is actually saving Mayview taxpayers a lot of money."

Everyone cheered except me. I grabbed the back of Mr. Ficken's wheelchair. My fingers ached. But I couldn't let go. "Gilbert," I whispered.

He didn't hear me. He was pouring drinks. Were there caterpillars in those cups? I couldn't tell.

Mitch tapped my arm.

"Look at Jolly," he said. "She looks strange."

Jolly stood next to her aunt. Except she was sort of swaying. She wiped her forehead. The sun felt stronger now. Then, just as Mom was about to give Ms. Van Pelt her award, Jolly sank to the ground.

"Help, someone," Ms. Van Pelt shouted. "My niece has fainted." She began fanning Jolly's face with her handkerchief.

"Get back," someone yelled.

"Give her air," a man said.

"Get a doctor," Jolly's aunt called out.

Mitch, Boom Boom, and I ran and helped Jolly to her feet. Mr. Marshall snapped our picture.

Mr. Ficken stepped out of his wheelchair, and Jolly flopped into it.

"Here," a woman said, reaching into Gilbert's wagon. She grabbed the nearest cup of punch. "Drink this," she said. "You'll feel better."

"Give that back," Gilbert said. "My caterpillar punch costs twenty-five cents a cup."

"Caterpillars," another woman screamed. "Look out, there are caterpillars in that punch."

"They're crawling all over the wagon and into the cups," someone else said.

A boy tipped Gilbert's wagon.

"Get your hands off," he said, pushing the boy.

Mitch and Boom Boom grabbed the pitchers as they hit the ground.

A crowd formed around us.

I grabbed Gilbert. "Bratski," I said, "let Jolly have some punch."

He shook his head and stomped his foot. "No way," he said. "She called me Gilbrat."

Jolly looked pale and dazed.

"Forget that," I said. "This is an emergency."

Jolly held out her hand. "Let me have it," she said.

Gilbert thought for a second. "Okey-dokey," he said, tossing the punch in her face.

The crowd gasped. But that did the trick. In a minute Jolly was back to her old self.

"How dare you," she sputtered. She ran her fingers through her hair and looked down at her blouse. There was

a big splat of greenish brown punch on it. Her blue and yellow ribbons drooped over her ears.

Gilbert stuck out his hand. "You owe me twenty-five cents," he said. "Pay up."

"I will not," she said, shaking her head.

Now Dr. Kugel was at Jolly's side. "Sorry," he said. "My beeper went off." He checked Jolly's pulse. "You'll be okay now," he said.

A nurse handed Jolly some orange juice and a towel.

"Did you have breakfast this morning?" Ms. Van Pelt asked Jolly.

Jolly shook her head. "Please don't tell my parents," she said. "It'll ruin their vacation."

Ms. Van Pelt put her arm around Jolly's shoulders. "All right," she said, "but no more silly business."

Jolly nodded and sipped her juice.

Ms. Van Pelt handed Gilbert a quarter. "Let's get on with the awards," she said.

I grabbed Gilbert's collar. "Say you're sorry," I said.

"She said to let her have it," Gilbert said. "It's her own fault."

"Gilbert," I said.

"I'm sorry, Jolly," he said in a tiny voice. "But only if you quit calling me Gilbrat."

Jolly wrinkled her nose. "All right," she said, stepping out of Mr. Ficken's wheelchair. "Actually, I feel much cooler now. I feel sorry for the rest of you."

We laughed.

All except Gilbert.

"What's up?" I asked him.

He stuck out his lower lip. "I only sold one cup of punch," he said. "Plus

I lost my caterpillars." He looked at me as if I was supposed to crawl around and find them.

"There's nothing I can do," I said.

Gilbert sniffed.

I turned away. Mom was getting ready to speak again.

"Ingrid Van Pelt and Fred Ficken work hard to make Mayview a better place to live," she began.

While Mom told everyone why they were such great neighbors, I secretly checked around for caterpillars.

Roe nudged me as Mom handed the medals to the Good Neighbors of the Year.

Mr. Marshall took their picture under our Silas G. Mayview poster.

After the awards, Zoe, the owner of Last Licks Ice Cream Parlor, gave us coupons for free ice cream. I couldn't wait to get some.

"What's your flavor of the month?" Zoe asked Jolly and Boom Boom.

Jolly leaned toward the microphone. "Jolly's Delight," she screeched. "Peppermint ice cream with rainbow sprinkles."

We covered our ears.

Boom Boom grabbed the mike. "With lots of nuts and a cherry on top." He raised his hands over his head.

Everyone applauded.

Zoe passed the microphone to me.

I wasn't sure what to say. "Well," I began. "Mr. Ficken's favorite flavor is butter pecan. We all like chocolate sprinkles," I said, pointing to my friends.

"And the name?" Zoe asked.

We were so busy with everything else, we never did think of a name.

"Oh boy," Gilbert said, squatting down. He reached behind a man's leg.

"I found one." He picked up a caterpillar and carefully put it into his box. He looked up at me and grinned.

I gave him a thumbs-up. That was when it hit me.

"We're calling our flavor Caterpillar Crunch," I said.

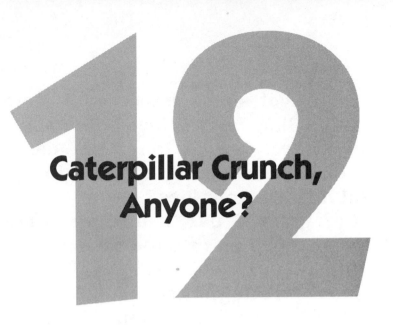

Caterpillar Crunch, Anyone?

After the ceremony, reporters crowded around Mom.

"Great idea to have the awards at the hospital, Mayor," a reporter said. "Was it a last-minute decision?"

"Yes," my mother said. "Our community has great spirit."

I felt drops of sweat running down my back. Just a few more steps and we would be in the car. I walked faster.

Dr. Kugel shook hands with Mom. "Looks like Busy's idea worked out well for everyone. So long," he said.

"Busy," Mom said, turning to me. "All this was your idea?"

Dad grabbed us. "I need air conditioning. Let's get into the car."

Uh oh, here it comes.

Mom got into the backseat with me.

"I feel like the chauffeur," Dad said, starting the car. He turned around and winked at me.

Mom faced me. "Tell me everything," she said.

First I took a deep breath of the cool air. Then I quickly told Mom about my call to Dr. Kugel and the newspaper. "Face it, Mom. If I asked you first you would have checked with a bunch of people. We didn't have much time. And Jolly was on my case."

Mom buckled her safety belt. "That's

beside the point, Busy," she said. "We've talked about this before. You've got to check with me first. This could have been very embarrassing."

"I know," I said, rubbing my clammy palms together. "I tried to find the right time to tell you." I shrugged. "I don't know what's wrong with me, Mom," I said, throwing up my hands. "It's just the way I am." Dad honked at some birds sitting in the lane.

Mom shook her head. Then she laughed.

She pulled off her pearl earrings and slipped them into her purse. She had her ears pierced when she was eighteen.

"There's nothing wrong with the way you are," she said.

"There isn't?" I said, beginning to smile.

She nodded. "Well, most of the time

anyway," she said, holding out her arms.

I couldn't lean over too far. The seat belt pressed into my side. But I didn't care. Right then I wouldn't have traded being the Mayor's daughter for anything.

Mom pushed some hair behind my ears. "And I'll tell you a secret," she said, taking my hand in hers. "When I was your age, I knew a girl who was a lot like Jolly. Today she's a very nice person."

"Who is she?" I asked.

"Ingrid Van Pelt," Mom said.

I laughed. "That figures."

Suddenly Dad stopped the car.

Mom and I looked out the window.

We were in front of Last Licks Ice Cream Parlor.

"Anyone for Caterpillar Crunch?" Dad asked.

"Way to go, Dad," I said, opening the door. "Can we stop for pizza too?"

"Might as well go for it," Dad said.

We brought the pizza home and ate it on the back steps.

After my parents went in, I stayed outside and waited for Roe. She was coming for a sleep over. I was flipping through *The History of Mayview* when I felt something brush my leg. I jumped.

"Gilbert," I said. "Does your mother know you're here?"

"Sure," he said. "I got permission."

I looked into the Bratskis' backyard. Mrs. Bratski waved.

"Send him back soon, Busy. He's all wound up after today."

"All right, Mrs. Bratski," I said. "He can stay for a while."

"Yahoo," Gilbert whooped, hopping on one foot.

"Come here and sit down," I said.

For once he did what I asked.

"Look at that," I said, pointing to a nearby flower bush.

"Huh, what?" he said.

"Shush, just look," I said. A beautiful black and yellow butterfly landed on the bush. "Remember Roe said that caterpillars turn into butterflies?"

He nodded and slipped his sticky hand into mine. "Do you think that butterfly was one of my caterpillars?"

"It's possible," I said.

"I bet it was," Gilbert said. "It looks a little familiar."

The air was still, and it smelled very sweet.

I squeezed his hand.

"I wish we saw him change into a butterfly," Gilbert said. "How did he do it?"

I shrugged and scratched my neck.

"Let's get a book about caterpillars at the library," I said. "We'll be experts."

"Good," Gilbert said, leaning back against the step. "After, we'll get Caterpillar Crunch cones."

"All right," I said, slapping him five. "Come on," I said. "We'll go out front and wait for Roe."

"I'll tell her about the butterfly," Gilbert said. He looked up at me. "Do you think I'm important, Busy?"

I nodded. "Sure, to your family and friends," I said.

"That makes me feel good," he said grinning.

"I'm glad," I told him, flicking a twig out of his hair.

Later that night Roe and I were on my bed in my room. Roe had brought sample nail polishes for us to try.

I painted my left hand Misty Rose and my right Lavender Lily.

Then we polished each other's toes.

My Mayview book was open on the bed.

"Silas G. Mayview looks like a nice guy," I said, covering a yawn.

Roe nodded and slid down under my spare blanket. "Maybe some of his relatives still live in Mayview," she said.

"We could find out," I said, wiggling my lavender toes.

"Can't it wait until morning? I'm pooped."

"Sure," I laughed.

"G'night, Busy."

"Night, Roe." I was just about to close the book when I saw a drawing of the Silas G. Mayview family tree. Something caught my eye. It was Silas Mayview's middle name.

The G stood for Gilbert.

Silas Gilbert Mayview.

Was this what Gilbert meant about

being important? He never did say the name of his famous relative. I flipped to Silas G. Mayview's picture. There was something familiar about those sticky-out ears. I sucked in a deep breath and looked at Roe. She was snoring softly. I didn't dare wake her.

Leaning over, I pulled away my curtains and looked out the window at the Bratskis' house. All their lights were out.

Was my Gilbert "The Brat" Bratski related to Mayview's founding father?

There was only one way to find out.
And I would.
For sure.
First thing.
Tomorrow.